BUSY TIMMY

By Kathryn and Byron Jackson
Illustrated by June Goldsborough

A GOLDEN BOOK, NEW YORK
Western Publishing Company, Inc., Racine, Wisconsin 53404

TIMMY is a big boy.

He can put on his outdoor clothes
all by himself.

He goes down the steps
with his big pail and shovel.

He climbs into his sandbox all by himself.
No one has to help him.
He's a big boy now.

A robin sees Timmy and comes flying.

A squirrel sees Timmy and comes running.

A rabbit sees Timmy and comes hopping.

They all watch Timmy
make little holes and big hills
in the cool white sand.

Timmy rides his horse
all around the flower bed.

Around and around he goes,
then back home again.

He goes up the steps
and opens the door
all by himself.

Timmy gets ready for his bath.
No one has to help him.
He's a big boy now.

He splashes in the bathtub
and sails his new boat.

He puts on
his own bib . . .

and holds
his own cup.

He eats all his supper with no help at all.

Timmy brushes
his teeth . . .

and climbs into bed, all by himself!

"Hush!" says the robin.
"Hush!" says the squirrel.
"Shush!" says the rabbit.

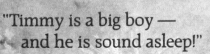

"Timmy is a big boy —
and he is sound asleep!"

Yes, Timmy is a big boy.
You are big, too.
Timmy does a lot of things.
So can you!